The Adventure Continues . . .

Hi! I'm Jackie. I'm an archaeologist. I study ancient treasures to learn how people lived in the past.

My big adventure started when I found a golden shield in Bavaria, Germany. I brought it back to my uncle's antique shop in San Francisco, California.

In the center of the shield was an eight-sided stone. It had a picture of a red rooster on it.

Uncle says the stone is a magical talisman. There are eleven more talismans, scattered across the globe. Each one has a different kind of magic.

All twelve talismans together have incredible power!

An evil group called The Dark Hand wants to use the power of the talismans to rule the world!

That's why I have to keep the rooster talisman away from them.

And it won't be easy.

They already tried to steal it from me once—and now they're back!

A PARACHUTE PRESS BOOK

Published by Grosset & Dunlap, a division of Penguin Putnam Books for Young Readers, New York. GROSSET & DUNLAP is a trademark of Penguin Putnam, Inc. Published simultaneously in Canada. Printed in U.S.A.

Library of Congress Cataloging-in-Publication Data is available.

ISBN 0-448-42650-1
A B C D E F G H I J

JACKIE CHAN
ADVENTURES ™ #2

Jade's
Secret Power

A novelization by Cathy West
based on the teleplay "The Power Within"
written by David Slack

Grosset & Dunlap

Chapter 1

"Chinese food! I don't want Chinese food," Jade complained. She frowned at the House of Wu menu. "I'm not in Hong Kong anymore. I'm in America! How about a hamburger? Or a hot dog?" She smiled at Jackie.

But Jackie Chan was too busy to notice. He was studying the small eight-sided talisman on the table. His old uncle stared at it, too.

"Jackie," Uncle said gravely, "the

rooster talisman is magical. It has great power."

Jade scooped up the talisman and looked at it. It had a picture of a rooster on one side. "What does it do?" she asked.

"*Manners,* Jade," Jackie said. He took the talisman from her hand. Then he placed it back on the table.

Jade sighed. America is supposed to be a lot more fun than this, she thought.

She slumped in her chair and stared down at her lap.

She didn't see what happened next. Nobody did.

The rooster on the stone talisman suddenly glowed!

It burned red like fire. Just for a

moment. Then it faded back to normal again.

Uncle was holding up his table place mat. Pictures of animals lined the edges. A pig, a monkey, a cow, a snake . . . there were a dozen animals in all, the symbols of the Chinese zodiac.

"Ancient legend speaks of twelve talismans," Uncle said. "One for each animal of the Chinese zodiac. Each talisman has a different magic. They—"

"What *kind* of magic?" Jade asked.

"Jade, Uncle wasn't finished speaking," Jackie pointed out.

Jade frowned and folded her arms across her chest.

Uncle straightened his glasses and

continued. "Legend says the twelve ancient talismans were scattered to the four corners of the globe. We must guard this one very carefully. It must never leave our sight. If this talisman—or any of the others—should fall into evil hands—"

"Jackie will give them smackie! With his lightning fists of steel!" Jade laughed.

Then she jumped up from her seat and chopped at the air. She tried to copy Jackie's martial arts moves. She slammed her fists on the table.

The dishes on the table clattered.

Jackie caught a teapot just before it crashed to the floor.

"Oops. Sorry," Jade said. She put the teapot and dishes back in place.

"When are you going to teach me some of your moves, Jackie?"

"Not now, Jade. Maybe later."

"Hummph!" Jade frowned. Later. Jackie *always* says later, she thought. I want something exciting to happen. *Right now!*

Jackie grabbed the rooster talisman. "Uncle, do you believe the legend?"

"Hey, Jackie, check me out!" Jade cried. She wanted him to pay some attention to her.

Jade danced across the restaurant floor. She kicked, punched, and karate-chopped the air.

Someone in the restaurant giggled. Other people stared.

"I've got the moves!" Jade shouted.

"Jade!" Jackie cried. "Not indoors!"

5

But Jade didn't listen. He'll see that I've got what it takes, she thought.

Jade kicked one leg high in the air. By accident she hit a waiter who was carrying a tray of food.

"Whoa!" The waiter stumbled into a table. His fall sent a big bowl of noodles flying up into the air. . . .

And the bowl landed right on Uncle's head.

Uncle was so startled, he fell out of his chair and knocked over the candle on the table.

The tablecloth burst into flames.

"Fire!" Jackie gasped. He quickly put out the fire with a big glass of water.

Uncle was sitting on the floor. He yanked the bowl off his head and tossed it over his shoulder.

No one saw the bowl land on Jade's spoon.

No one saw the spoon hit the magical talisman.

No one saw the magical talisman soar into the air. . . .

The magical talisman flew across the room. It soared toward three bowls of steaming noodle soup set out on a serving tray.

Splash!

It landed in one of the bowls of soup. Someone was in for a surprise with their meal!

7

Chapter 2

Jade, Jackie, and Uncle returned to their seats.

A waiter picked up the serving tray and brought them their soup. Jade's bowl had the talisman hidden inside.

"Sorry, Jackie," Jade said. "I was just trying to get you to teach me some of your moves."

Jackie leaned forward. He stared into Jade's eyes. "The wise seek power within themselves. The foolish seek it within others. Until you can control the power within yourself, I cannot teach you."

"Huh? What does that mean?" Jade asked.

Jackie sighed. "It means you must have the discipline to behave yourself," he told Jade. "Now eat your food."

"'Power within' . . ." Jade muttered. "Got it." She grabbed her spoon and began to slurp up her soup.

Jackie rolled his eyes. "Don't eat like a baboon," he said. "Chew your food slowly."

"*Chew* soup?" Jade asked. She took another long slurp. And another. "No one chews soup!"

Jade picked up her bowl. With one giant gulp, she drained the rest of her soup.

Jade felt the noodles slide down her throat. But she did not feel the talisman slide down with them.

She burped and set the bowl on the table with a thump. "Not bad," she said.

Jackie didn't say a word. He just shook his head.

The waiter placed a small plate of fortune cookies on the table.

Jade clapped her hands. "Oooh! Dessert!" she cried.

She broke open a cookie and pulled out the tiny fortune.

"'Danger looms in your future,'" she read out loud.

Uncle nodded. "Yes. We must be very careful."

"Uncle, you don't really listen to cookies, do you?" Jackie asked.

Before Uncle could answer, three men came up to the table. Their names were Finn, Ratso, and Chow.

"Good evening, Chan," Finn said.

Jade gasped. She knew these men. They belonged to the The Dark Hand—an evil group who wanted to rule the world!

Uncle glanced at the men. Then he looked at Jackie. "You see? Danger," he said. "The cookie was right!"

"Where is the talisman?" Finn wanted to know.

Before Jackie could say a word, Finn lifted a chair and came after him.

11

But Jackie knocked the chair aside.

Uncle rose from his seat. He picked up a broom leaning against a wall. With a slight flick of his wrist, he whacked Ratso.

Ratso stumbled to the ground.

"Wow!" Jade cried. "Go, Uncle!"

"I'm out of here!" Chow said. He ran for the door.

Ratso and Finn rushed out, too.

"Thank you for dining with us!" Jackie called after them.

Jade giggled. Jackie and Uncle were so cool!

"Oh, no! Where is it?" Jackie said.

Jade watched Jackie search the table. He looked under plates. He even looked inside the teapot.

"The talisman!" he cried. "It's gone!"

He turned toward the door. "The Dark Hand must have taken it!"

"Come on! We can catch 'em!" Jade started to race outside.

But Jackie caught her by the hood of her red sweatshirt.

"No. Stay with Uncle," he ordered. "It's too dangerous. The talisman has fallen into the hands of evil. I must get it back—before it's too late."

Chapter 3

Finn, Ratso, and Chow stopped in an alley to catch their breath. They also had to call Valmont, their boss.

Finn pulled out his video phone. It was a cell phone with a video screen on it.

Chow glanced at the video phone. "We didn't get the talisman," he said.

"Valmont is not going to be happy about this." Ratso started to shake. "Maybe we shouldn't call him."

Suddenly, Valmont's face appeared on the tiny screen. "Do you have the talisman?" he asked.

Finn swallowed. "Uh, not yet, Mr. Valmont, sir. It didn't go quite as planned."

"Tell me," Valmont said.

"Well, we stomped Chan," Finn lied. "But we didn't find the rooster talisman."

Valmont sighed. "You will all be punished."

Finn shivered with fear as Valmont's face disappeared from the screen.

Back at The Dark Hand's head-quarters, Valmont was very angry.

He looked at the stone statue behind him. It was shaped like a

15

dragon. The statue held the evil spirit of Shendu, the real leader of The Dark Hand.

"They could not find the talisman," he told Shendu.

"Do not worry, Valmont," the evil spirit whispered. "Perhaps the blind can be made to see . . . with the eyes of a dragon."

Shendu's eyes flashed red.

A glowing object magically appeared at Valmont's feet. It was a large, fancy wand. At the top of the wand were four red-eyed dragons.

Each dragon pointed in a different direction. North, south, east, west.

"Use The Seeker to find the talisman," Shendu whispered. "Its eyes can see all."

Dozens of ninjas quickly fluttered into the room. The warriors were all dressed in black. They were the Shadowkhan.

One of them closed his hand around The Seeker. Then, with the speed of lightning, the Shadowkhan disappeared into the shadows.

Valmont's lips curved into an evil smile. The Shadowkhan will not fail, he thought.

Jackie dashed out of the House of Wu and raced into the alley.

Jade ran out behind him. She peeked around the corner to spy on him.

"Stay with Uncle?" she whispered to herself. "No way! Besides, Jackie didn't say *which* uncle!"

Just ahead, Jackie saw Valmont's men. They jumped into their car and sped away.

Jackie stopped running. A chill ran down his back. He suddenly had a strange feeling. As if someone was behind him.

Lurking silently in the shadows were the Shadowkhan. They watched Jackie's every move.

But when Jackie whirled around, the street was empty.

"Hmm." Jackie shrugged and took off after the car.

Just then, Jade crept out from her hiding place. She suddenly had a strange feeling, too. As if someone was behind *her!*

She whirled around.

The street was empty.

"Hmm." Jade shrugged and raced after Jackie.

She screamed when two strong hands grabbed her and dragged her into the darkness.

Chapter 4

"Let me go!" Jade cried out. She turned to see who was holding her—and gasped.

It was Jackie.

"Um . . . hi!" Jade said.

"I can't believe you followed me," Jackie said. "What do you *hear* when I talk? Tell me, does it sound like this? Blah blah blah, blah-blah-blah-blah?"

Jade grinned. "Sorry." But then

her eyes grew wide. "Um, Jackie. We're not alone." She grabbed his arm.

Jackie turned—and saw the Shadowkhan! The alley was filled with them.

He picked up Jade and tucked her under his arm like a football. Then he started to run.

"Why are we running away?" she asked Jackie. "Aren't you going to whomp 'em?"

"Ancient Chinese proverb," Jackie gasped as he ran. "Do not fight when you can run!"

They reached the corner, and Jackie stopped running. He set Jade down. Then he pointed down the street. "You go that way!"

"But—" Jade began.

"Go!" Jackie insisted. "They'll chase after me. You will be safer away from me!"

Jade's shoulders slumped. "Oh, all right." She ran the way her uncle pointed.

Jackie raced away in the opposite direction. He glanced back at the Shadowkhan.

Hey! What was going on? The Shadowkhan were not chasing *him.*

They were chasing Jade!

Jade gasped for breath. She looked over her shoulder.

The Shadowkhan were right behind her!

"Why are they chasing *me?*" she cried. She ran as fast as she could.

But it wasn't fast enough. The Shadowkhan were getting closer!

"I bet I can lose them on this!" Jade slid to a stop in front of a trash can, where she saw a beaten-up skateboard and an old blue helmet sticking out of the garbage.

She strapped on the helmet and took off.

"Yes!" Jade shouted as she flew down a hill.

Jackie reached the top of the hill just in time to see that his niece was in trouble.

The army of Shadowkhan had jumped onto the roof of a speeding truck. And the truck was closing in on Jade!

Jackie saw a man rolling an empty

shopping cart down the street.

He quickly grabbed the cart and jumped inside. "Sorry-I'll-bring-it-right-back-thank you!" he cried out to the man.

Jackie surfed down the hill in the cart. He had to distract the Shadowkhan so that Jade could get away!

He raced toward the truck as fast as he could. Cars honked as he dodged through the traffic. But Jackie was getting closer to the truck with the Shadowkhan on top of it. He was almost there. Then—

Beeeeeeeep!

A taxicab was headed straight for Jackie.

"Oh, no!" Jackie cried. He tried to swerve out of the way, but he couldn't.

Jackie leaped off the cart. He sailed through the air—and landed on the truck that carried the Shadowkhan.

Before Jackie could catch his breath, the Shadowkhan attacked him. He fought them off one by one.

Now Jade will be safe, Jackie thought, blocking punches.

He knocked a strange wand from the hand of one of the Shadowkhan.

It fell over the side of the truck.

At the same time, a giant of a man was standing in the street, watching them. He was as tall and wide as ten grown men. His name was Tohru. He worked for The Dark Hand.

He watched as The Seeker flew out of the hand of a Shadowkhan.

Tohru reached up and caught The Seeker. He held the wand high in the air.

The eyes of one of the dragons glowed.

Now Tohru knew which way to go. He knew just how to find where the rooster talisman was hidden.

Still on her skateboard, Jade reached the bottom of the hill. But she was headed straight for a crew of workers on the Golden Gate Bridge.

She was going too fast to stop!

Her skateboard rolled onto one of the workmen's ramps and whooshed up, up, up . . .

And went flying straight off the bridge!

"Nooooooooo!" Jade screamed. Her skateboard flew out from under her.

Then something strange happened.

"Huh?" Jade looked down. She kicked her feet.

She wasn't falling into the water!

She was floating in the air.

Like magic!

Jade's heart pounded. How is this possible? she wondered. I'm standing in midair.

Jade walked on air back to the bridge. "How did I *do* that?" she wondered.

But there was no time to think about it.

Screeech! Truck tires squealed on the road.

The truck carrying Jackie and the

Shadowkhan was heading straight for her!

With a loud crash, the truck hit the bridge. Jackie and the Shadow-khan sailed over its railing.

Jackie dangled from the bridge by his fingertips. He struggled back up to safety, but the Shadowkhan fell into the water below.

"Jackie!" Jade cried. "The coolest thing ever just happened! I went right off the bridge. But I didn't fall. I stopped in midair. Then I ran back—just like in cartoons! I can fly!"

Jackie rolled his eyes. "Jade, we must be serious. The Dark Hand is after you. And I don't know why!"

An enormous hand fell on Jackie's shoulder and squeezed it hard. Jackie

29

slumped to the ground.

"Jackie!" Jade cried. She kneeled next to him. He was out cold!

Jade's knees trembled as she looked up, up, up . . . at a mountain of a man.

It was Tohru.

Tohru pointed The Seeker at her. The dragon's eyes glowed.

Jade drew back. What was that thing?

The giant held out a hand. "The talisman," he demanded. "Give it to me."

"I—I don't have it!" Jade stuttered. "*You* guys have it . . . don't you?"

Back at The Dark Hand head-quarters, Valmont paced in front of

Shendu. He was waiting to hear from Tohru and the Shadowkhan.

Soon he would have the rooster talisman. Soon he would possess its power!

Valmont's video phone rang. He clicked it on. Tohru's face filled the entire screen.

"The Seeker points to the girl," Tohru said. "But I searched her. She does not have the talisman."

Valmont glared at the screen. "Well, it must be hidden on her *some-where,* Tohru!" he said. "I'm sure she didn't *eat* it."

Valmont suddenly froze. "Or *did* she?" he added.

Valmont turned to Shendu.

"Man *is* much wiser when he

looks *within*," the spirit hissed.

Valmont nodded. He turned back to Tohru. "Get the talisman," he said. "No matter what it takes."

Tohru listened. "I understand, master."

"And while you're at it," Valmont added, "get rid of Jackie Chan!"

Chapter 6

"Let me out of this place!" Jade screamed.

She was strapped to a table in some kind of building. Tohru had taken her and Jackie there. From the way it smelled, she guessed it was a fish factory. Yuck!

Jade struggled against the leather straps, but she couldn't move.

Across the room, Jackie was handcuffed to a pole. Jade called to him, but he was still out cold.

"Helloooo! Let me out of here!" Jade shouted again. "I mean it! Just wait till the Jackinator wakes up! You guys are gonna get so *creamed!*"

Suddenly, Jackie groaned. He shook his head. His eyes opened just as Tohru thudded into the room.

Jackie struggled against his handcuffs. He twisted and turned. But he couldn't pull his hands free.

Tohru stepped up to Jade. He held The Seeker over her head. Nothing happened.

What is he doing? Jade wondered.

Tohru moved The Seeker slowly over her body. He stopped when he reached her tummy—and all four dragon heads glowed.

"Aha!" Tohru said.

"Aha *what?*" Jade shouted. She was worried. But she tried not to show it.

Tohru raised a huge sword. Its giant curved blade glinted in the light.

"W-W-What are you going to do with *that?*" Jade squeaked.

Tohru gave her an evil grin. Then he aimed the blade right at her belly button!

Chapter 7

Jade closed her eyes tightly. Her heart pounded as she waited to see what Tohru would do next.

She heard a loud squeal and opened her eyes.

Tohru was no longer hovering over her. He stood at the other end of the room.

"Yes!" Jade cheered.

But then she saw what Tohru was doing.

Jade gasped. He was sharpening the sword!

She suddenly realized what Tohru was going to do.

And she suddenly realized *why!*

"Jackie!" Jade called out. "The rooster talisman is in my stomach! I must have swallowed it at the restaurant!"

Jade thought back to the restaurant. Back to what Uncle had said there: *"The rooster talisman is magical. It has great power."*

Then she remembered what happened at the Golden Gate Bridge. How she flew over the side. How she hung in midair.

Jade's eyes lit up. She knew just what to do. She had to use the magic of the talisman!

Jade pushed out her stomach.

She strained hard against the heavy belt that strapped her to the table.

"Grrrrrr!" She pushed and pushed.

Jackie was watching her. He gasped when boxes, cans, and crates began to float in the air—as if by magic!

"Jade," Jackie cried. "You can move things with your mind!"

"No," Jade said, grinning. "With my *stomach!*"

But her smile quickly faded as a huge, dark shadow fell over her.

Tohru was back!

He lifted his sharp sword over his head. "Hold still," he growled.

Jade glanced at the ceiling. High

above them, a giant crate hung from a chain.

Jade smiled. She had an idea.

She gritted her teeth. Then she squeezed her eyes closed. "Focus-focus-focus-focus-focus-focus," she mumbled.

Tohru stared at her. But Jade ignored him.

"Grrrrrr!" She was concentrating hard.

Tohru looked puzzled. "Why are you making that noise?"

"Here's why!" Jade shouted.

Crash!

The crate landed on top of Tohru.

Jade had used the power of the talisman to move it. And it knocked the giant out cold!

Hundreds of smelly fish spilled across the floor.

"I did it!" Jade cried. She grinned at her uncle. "I guess I have that 'power within' you were talking about," she told him.

"That's *not* what I meant." Jackie laughed. "Quick! Cut yourself free!

"Right!" Jade concentrated once more. Slowly, she lifted the sword from Tohru's hand. She made it fly over her and—

Chop! It cut through the straps that held her down.

Jade jumped down from the table and ran to free her uncle.

Just then, the door swung open.

Finn, Ratso, and Chow entered the room.

40

"Jade!" Jackie cried. "Run! Fly! Do something!"

His hands were still cuffed to the pole. He scooped her up with his legs and tossed her into the air.

"Whoa!" Jade flew like a bird toward the ceiling.

"Get the girl!" Finn ordered Ratso. Then he headed for Jackie.

Jackie tried to back away from Finn. But the handcuffs held him tight. He was trapped.

"You can't beat me without your hands, Chan," Finn said. He swung an arm at Jackie.

Jackie heard something rattle in Finn's pocket.

Were they the keys to his handcuffs?

Jackie ducked and dodged Finn's punches. When Ratso and Chow came to help Finn, Jackie slipped a few fingers into Finn's pocket. He grabbed the keys—and set himself free!

Jackie fought off Finn, Ratso, and Chow. Then he heard an angry roar!

Tohru had woken up under the mountain of fish. "I *hate* fish!" he yelled.

Jade flew just above Jackie's shoulder. "Uh . . . why fight when you can run? Isn't that what you said, Jackie?"

"You're learning!" Jackie shouted.

Jade zoomed through the air. "This way!" She led her uncle to a staircase.

Jackie followed her up to a room on the second floor.

Seconds later, Tohru's huge body filled the doorway.

Jackie and Jade dashed toward another door. But Tohru threw a heavy crate. It crashed against the door, blocking their exit.

"What do you do when you can't run?" Jade asked her uncle.

"Don't watch," Jackie replied grimly.

"Rrraaaaaaaaaa!" Tohru boomed. He ran toward Jackie.

Jackie tried to fight him off, but the giant was too strong.

Tohru grabbed Jackie and held him in a headlock.

"Jackie!" Jade cried. She had to

help her uncle somehow.

Jade looked around the room. I've got to hit Tohru with the biggest thing I can find, she thought. But what?

Then she grinned. The biggest thing was Tohru himself!

Jade focused on Tohru as hard as she could.

Slowly, the huge man rose into the air like a giant balloon.

"Huh?" he said as he floated toward the ceiling. He dropped Jackie to the floor.

Tohru rose higher and higher.

Jade strained with all her might to keep the giant in the air. "Can't hold him . . . much longer . . ." she groaned.

With a huge gasp she let Tohru drop.

Tohru smashed a big hole right through the wooden floor. And Jackie fell into the hole with him!

Down, down they fell—through two more floors. Then they plunged into the river that flowed beneath the fish factory.

Jade flew out of the building and to the river.

She quickly spotted Tohru. He was bobbing like a whale in the waters below. But where was Jackie?

Then she saw him. Jackie was safe on land.

Jade sighed with relief. He was sitting at the edge of the water. She flew to his side.

"Hey," she said. "Sorry."

Jackie didn't reply. He rubbed his sore arm as he climbed to his feet.

Was he angry with her?

Then Jackie motioned to Jade to follow him.

Jade sighed again.

This is probably my last adventure with Jackie, she thought glumly. I've caused so much trouble, I bet now he'll send me home to Hong Kong.

46

Chapter 8

Jackie and Jade went to a secret place called Section Thirteen. There, Jackie tried to explain things to Captain Augustus Black.

Captain Black was the head of Section Thirteen. It was a special law enforcement agency. Jackie was helping Black stop the evil crimes of The Dark Hand.

"I'm telling you, Uncle was right. The talismans *do* possess magic powers," Jackie said. "I saw it myself!"

Black nodded. But Jackie could tell he didn't believe him.

"Of course they have powers, Jackie. Now why don't you get some sleep?" Black opened a door.

Jackie stepped through.

"Whoa!" Jackie couldn't believe what he saw. The room looked just like his apartment above Uncle's antique shop. It was filled with all of Jackie's belongings.

"All my stuff!" he said. "How did it get here?"

"Until we can defeat The Dark Hand, it is safer for you to live here at Section Thirteen," Black explained. He patted Jackie on the shoulder. "I hope it feels like home."

"But . . . what about Uncle?" Jackie asked.

"Your uncle refused to move." Black shrugged.

Jackie nodded. "Uncle is very stubborn."

Another door in the room opened. A man and a woman entered. They were two of Black's agents. They had Jade with them.

"Jade's stomach was successfully pumped," the male agent announced. "We found the rooster talisman."

The female agent patted Jade on the shoulder.

Jade grabbed her stomach. She looked a little sick. "Cock-a-doodle-doo," she mumbled.

"What about my niece, Jade?" Jackie

whispered to Black. "Where will she stay?"

Captain Black pointed to a pile of stuff in the corner. Suitcases, teddy bears, a heart pillow . . .

"Yes!" Jade cheered when she saw her things. Suddenly, she felt much better. But then she stopped. She looked at Jackie. "Can I stay?" she asked. "You're not mad at me . . . are you?"

Jackie kneeled down beside her. "Of course you can stay," he said. "And no. I'm not angry."

"Allllllrrrrright!" Jade cheered. "I'm not going back to Hong Kong! I'm staying with Jackie!"

She gave him a big hug, and jumped around the room.

"Yippee! Yahoo! Hurray!" she cried.

Jackie groaned.

Black smiled. "I trust you'll keep your niece in check."

"Does this mean I'm a secret agent now?" Jade asked.

"No!" Black and Jackie both shouted at once.

But Jade grinned.

She had her own ideas about that.

They didn't call it *secret* agent for nothing!

A letter to you from Jackie

Dear Friends,

   In <u>Jade's Secret Power</u>, Jade wants me to teach her all of my martial arts moves right away. She thinks she is ready to learn everything. But she's not ready. Not yet, anyway.

   That's why I tell her: the wise seek power within themselves. The foolish seek it within others.

   Lots of my young friends tell me, "Jackie, I want to be just like you when I grow up." I love that! I am honored to be a role model to so many kids.

   I know that Jade thinks it's cool when she sees me fight off the bad guys from The Dark Hand. But I'd like Jade and my fans to remember that what is natural for me may not be right for anybody else. Each person is special and should never forget to be him or herself above all else.

   I learned this secret years ago, when I first started making movies. Back then, directors told me that I should act just like another kung fu artist. His name was Bruce Lee.

   I thought Bruce Lee was the greatest. I respected his martial arts skills as well as his acting talent. He was also very famous, and I looked up to him as a role model.

I tried my best to be exactly like Bruce. But nobody liked my movies. They kept saying that I was no Bruce Lee. Of course not, I thought. I'm Jackie! I have my own style. I am my own person. That is what I needed to show people.

Right then, I made a big decision. I was never going to pretend to be someone else again. And my next movie was a big success. Everyone got to see my funny side and my own martial arts style.

So, it's great to have someone you look up to. But you don't have to be exactly like him or her. It's always better to be exactly like you!

Find out what happens in the next book

#3 Sign of the Ox

Jackie is on a hunt to find the ox talisman. The problem is the mightiest wrestler in Mexico has it. There is no way he is going to give it to Jackie without a fight!

Enter the

JACKIE CHAN ADVENTURES™

Ultimate Fan Sweepstakes!
— NO PURCHASE NECESSARY —

Are you the Ultimate Fan?
**Enter today and you could be a lucky winner of one
of the following great *Jackie Chan Adventures* prizes:**

1 Grand Prize
Win a *Jackie Chan Adventures* Ultimate Fan Gift Pack!
Includes the first five Jackie Chan Adventures books autographed by Jackie Chan, T-shirt,
video, action figures, sticker activity pack, board game, backpack, video game,
and other cool *Jackie Chan Adventures* gifts!

5 First Prizes
Win the first five *Jackie Chan Adventures* books,
including an autographed copy of #1 THE DARK HAND!

50 Second Prizes
Win a copy of *Jackie Chan Adventures* #5 SHENDU ESCAPES!

Complete this entry form or hand print all of the information listed below
on a 3' x 5' card (see Official Rule #2) and send it to:

Jackie Chan Adventures Ultimate Fan Sweepstakes
Village Station
P. O. Box 1045
New York, NY 10014

Name _____

Address _____

City _____

State _____ **Zip** _____

Phone _____ **Birthdate** ___/___/___

Jackie Chan Adventures™ Ultimate Fan Sweepstakes Official Rules

1. **NO PURCHASE NECESSARY**. A purchase will not improve your chances of winning.

2. To enter complete the official entry form or hand print your name, address, age, and phone number along with the words "JACKIE CHAN ADVENTURES Ultimate Fan Sweepstakes" on a 3" x 5" card and mail to: JACKIE CHAN ADVENTURES Ultimate Fan Sweepstakes, Village Station, P. O. Box 1045, New York, NY 10014, postmarked **no later than January 31, 2002**. Enter as often as you wish, but each entry must be mailed separately. One entry per envelope. Partially completed, illegible, or mechanically reproduced entries will not be accepted. Sponsor is not responsible for lost, late, mutilated, illegible, stolen, postage due, incomplete, or misdirected entries. All entries become the property of Penguin Putnam Inc., and will not be returned.

3. The sweepstakes is open to legal residents of the United States and Canada (excluding Quebec), between the ages of five and twelve as of January 31, 2002, except as set forth below. Void in Puerto Rico and wherever prohibited or restricted by law. All federal, state, and local laws apply. In the event a winner is a Canadian resident, he or she must answer a time-limited skill question consisting of an arithmetical problem to be determined a winner. Sony Pictures Entertainment Inc., Kids' WB!, Adelaide Productions, Inc., Penguin Putnam Inc., Parachute Properties and Parachute Press, Inc. (individually and collectively "Parachute"), their respective officers, directors, shareholders, employees, suppliers, parents, subsidiaries, affiliates, agencies, sponsors, participating retailers, and persons connected with the use, marketing or conduct of this sweepstakes are not eligible. And family members living in the same household as any of the individuals referred to in the immediately forgoing sentence are not eligible.

4. Odds of winning depend on the total number of entries received. All prizes will be awarded. Winners will be randomly drawn on or about February 15, 2002, by Penguin Putnam Inc., whose decisions are final. Potential winners will be notified by mail and will be required to sign and return an affidavit of eligibility, release of liability, and all other legal documents which the sweepstakes sponsor may require (including a W-9 tax form) within 14 days of notification or an alternate winner will be selected. Prizes won by minors will be awarded to their parent or legal guardian who must sign and return all required legal documents. By acceptance of their prize, winners or winners' parents on winners' behalf consent to the use of their names, photographs, likeness, and personal information by Penguin Putnam, Parachute, Sony Pictures Entertainment, Adelaide, or Kids' WB!, and for any advertising, promotion, or publicity purposes without further compensation except where prohibited.

5. a) One (1) **Grand Prize Winner** wins a JACKIE CHAN ADVENTURES Ultimate Fan Gift Pack which includes the first five JACKIE CHAN ADVENTURES books autographed by Jackie Chan, T-shirt, video, action figures, board game, sticker activity pack, backpack, video game and other Jackie Chan Adventures product. Approximate retail value $100.00.

b) Five (5) **First Prize Winners** win the first five JACKIE CHAN ADVENTURES books, including an autographed copy of Book #1 THE DARK HAND. Approximate retail value $24.95.

c) Fifty (50) **Second Prize Winners** win a copy of JACKIE CHAN ADVENTURES Book #5 SHENDU ESCAPES. Approximate retail value $4.99.

6. Only one prize will be awarded per individual, family, or household. Prizes are non-transferable and cannot be sold or redeemed for cash. No cash substitute is available. Any federal, state, or local taxes are the responsibility of the winner. Sponsor may substitute prize of equal or greater value, if necessary, due to availability.

7. Additional terms: By participating, entrants agree a) to the official rules and decisions of the judges, which will be final in all respects; and to waive any claim to ambiguity of the official rules and b) to release, discharge, and hold harmless Penguin Putnam, Parachute, Sony Pictures Entertainment, Kids' WB!, Adelaide and their respective officers, directors, shareholders, employees, suppliers, parents, subsidiaries, affiliates, agencies, sponsors, participating retailers and persons connected with the use, marketing or conduct of this sweepstakes from and against any and all liability or damages associated with acceptance, use, or misuse of any prize received in this sweepstakes.

8. Any dispute arising from this sweepstakes will be determined according to the laws of the State of New York, without reference to its conflict of law principles, and the entrants consent to the personal jurisdiction of the State and Federal courts located in New York County and agree that such courts have exclusive jurisdiction over all such disputes.

9. To obtain the name of the winners, please send your request and a self-addressed stamped envelope to JACKIE CHAN ADVENTURES Ultimate Fan Sweepstakes, Village Station, P. O. Box 1045, New York, NY 10014 by March 1, 2002. Sweepstakes Sponsor: Penguin Putnam Inc.

YOU CAN JOIN JACKIE'S J TEAM

Monday through Saturday on **Kids' WB!** to get your J-Team challenge. After you complete a challenge go to **KidsWB.com** to win!

[Here's a hint: you've already completed a J-Team mind challenge by reading this book.]